Shall We Dance?

TAP DANCE

by Wendy Hinote Lanier

I0888904

FOCUS READERS

FOCUS READERS

www.focusreaders.com

Copyright © 2018 by Focus Readers, Lake Elmo, MN 55042. All rights reserved. No part of this book may be reproduced or utilized in any form or by any means without written permission from the publisher.

Focus Readers is distributed by North Star Editions:
sales@northstareditions.com | 888-417-0195

Produced for Focus Readers by Red Line Editorial.

Photographs ©: AndreasKermann/iStockphoto, cover, 1; Lorraine Swanson/Shutterstock Images, 4–5; SpeedKingz/Shutterstock Images, 6; RonHStock/iStockphoto, 9; antoniodiaz/Shutterstock Images, 10–11; StephanHoerold/iStockphoto, 12; Kirill Kallinikov/Sputnik/AP Images, 14–15, 29; ClaireMcAdams/iStockphoto, 17; Rus S/Shutterstock Images, 18; 4x6/iStockphoto, 21; Jack Delano/Farm Security Administration/Office of War Information Black-and-White Negatives/Library of Congress, 22–23; Pavel L Photo and Video/Shutterstock Images, 24; Kathy Willens/AP Images, 27

ISBN
978-1-63517-278-2 (hardcover)
978-1-63517-343-7 (paperback)
978-1-63517-473-1 (ebook pdf)
978-1-63517-408-3 (hosted ebook)

Library of Congress Control Number: 2017935125

Printed in the United States of America
Mankato, MN
June, 2017

About the Author

Wendy Hinote Lanier is a native Texan and former elementary teacher who writes and speaks for children and adults on a variety of topics. She is the author of more than 20 books for children and young people. Some of her favorite people are dogs.

TABLE OF CONTENTS

CHAPTER 1

IT'S TIME TO TAP

Imagine a dance that can be seen and heard. Tap dancers use their shoes as instruments. Each shoe has metal taps attached to the bottom. One tap covers the heel. Another covers the tip of the toe.

Tap dancing combines sound and movement.

People have been tap dancing for decades.

Hitting the taps against the floor creates a sound. Tap dancers play rhythms as they dance. They strike the floor in different ways. This creates different sounds.

Tap dancing began in the United States. It is a mix of different **percussion** dances. These include Irish jigs and English **clog** dances. Scottish **hornpipes** also influenced early forms of tap dancing. African tribal dances were influences, too.

DANCE TIP

Keep your knees slightly bent and your weight forward over your toes. Make sure your body moves with your feet.

Traveling **minstrel shows** were common in the late 1800s. Performers often danced an early form of tap dancing. It was called soft-shoe. **Vaudeville** shows had soft-shoe dancing, too. By the early 1920s, the first metal taps appeared. Soon tap dancing was a popular dance form. Tap dancers were featured in nightclubs. They were on **Broadway**. Sometimes they were even in movies.

Tap dancing is fun for all.

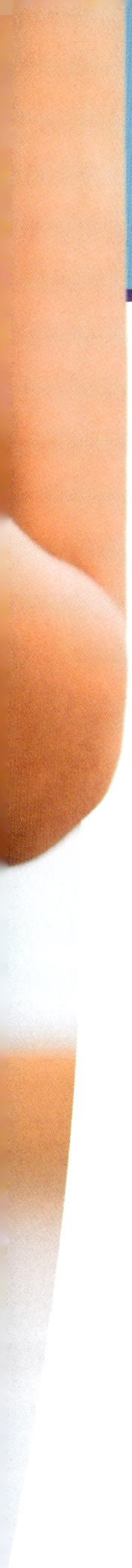

CHAPTER 2

DRESS TO MOVE

Tap dancers move a lot. They need clothes they can easily move in. Women tap dancers sometimes wear **leotards**. But jazz pants and a T-shirt are common for both men and women.

Practice clothes don't need to be fancy.

The right tap shoes can make all the difference.

Shoes are the most important part of tap dancing. They must be comfortable. And they must make a good sound.

Most dancers wear lace-up shoes. These shoes are leather. They have a low heel. Aluminum taps are screwed to the soles. Tap shoes can also be **customized**. Some dance techniques require more support. The taps can also be made to have different tones.

DANCE TIP

Hard leather shoes take longer to break in. But they last longer than soft leather.

МЮЗИКЛ
ПОЮЩИЕ
ПОД ДОЖДЕМ
МЮЗИКЛ
ПОЮЩИЕ
ПОД ДОЖДЕМ

CHAPTER 3

BASIC MOVES

Tap performances take a lot of energy. A good warm-up helps prevent injuries. Simply walk forward, backward, and sideways. Do it at different **tempos**.

A good warm-up will get you ready to perform.

Flaps and shuffles are basic steps. Every beginner must learn them before moving on to harder steps.

A flap is also called a brush step. It consists of two taps. First, tap by brushing the ball of your foot away from your body. Then make the

DANCE TIP

Tap dancing takes practice. Do each step slowly at first. Go faster as you master the step.

A tap dancer performs a traveling flap.

second tap. Do this by touching the ball of your foot to the floor. Leave the heel raised as you do this.

Tap dancing with your friends is a great way to learn the style.

A shuffle step also has two taps. It combines a brush to the front and a brush back. The step is done on one foot and then the other. The rhythm is slow at first. But it gets faster and faster.

DANCE TIP

Are you slipping in your tap shoes? Glue a piece of rubber on the sole between the taps.

TRY IT OUT

THE CRAMP-ROLL

A well-known tap step is the cramp-roll. One cramp-roll is four beats: toe, toe, heel, heel. Start with a right cramp-roll.

1. Step forward on the right toe-tap.
2. Step forward on the left toe-tap. Both heels should remain off the ground.
3. Drop the right heel.
4. Drop the left heel.

A left cramp-roll has the same steps. But it begins on the left foot.

A cramp-roll has four beats.

CHAPTER 4

ON WITH THE SHOW!

Tap dancing was once very popular in the United States. Its popularity began to decline in the 1950s. But the style never disappeared. And in the 1980s it made a comeback.

College students take part in a tap dancing class in 1942.

Tap dancers perform in a show.

Popular TV shows and movies showed tap dance. The style appeared on Broadway, too. In 1989, President George H. W. Bush even made May 25 National Tap Dance Day.

Savion Glover also played an important role. In 1984, he took over the starring role in *The Tap Dance Kid*. It was a popular Broadway show. Glover was only 10 years old. But he impressed fans with his fancy footwork. And he was just getting started.

DANCE TIP

Listen carefully to the music as you dance. Make sure to keep in time to the music.

Glover developed a style. It was based on funk and hip-hop. Glover often was on *Sesame Street*. He later became a **choreographer**. He choreographed the movie *Happy Feet*. His work has inspired a new generation of tap dancers.

Today tap dancing is often featured in popular shows. Young dancers usually start by learning the basics at a local dance studio. Some of the best dancers go on to appear in big shows.

Savion Glover helped make tap dance popular again.

They bring a fresh new style to these performances. Their work is inspiring many people to try it themselves. Tap dancing is a dance form that continues to grow and change.

FOCUS ON

TAP DANCING

Write your answers on a separate piece of paper.

1. Write a letter to a friend describing the main idea of Chapter 4.
2. What do you think is the most important part of choosing tap shoes? Why?
3. Where did Savion Glover perform as a tap dancer in *The Tap Dance Kid*?
   A. a traveling minstrel show
   B. a vaudeville act
   C. a Broadway show
4. What might happen if your dance shoes don't fit properly or if your feet don't have enough support?
   A. You might invent a new step.
   B. You might injure yourself.
   C. You might not make tapping sounds.

5. What does **rhythms** mean in this book?

*Tap dancers play **rhythms** as they dance. They strike the floor in different ways. This creates different sounds.*

- **A.** musical instruments
- **B.** musical patterns
- **C.** musical games

6. What does **decline** mean in this book?

*Tap dancing was once very popular in the United States. Its popularity began to **decline** in the 1950s. But the style never disappeared.*

- **A.** become less common
- **B.** become more common
- **C.** gain more attention

Answer key on page 32.

GLOSSARY

Broadway
An area in New York City where there are many theaters.

choreographer
A person who creates dance routines.

clog
A dance in which performers wear thick wooden shoes.

customized
Made or built for a particular person.

hornpipes
Lively dances that were a favorite of sailors.

leotards
Formfitting one-piece garments usually worn by dancers.

minstrel shows
Stage shows featuring singers, dancers, and comedians.

percussion
Instruments that produce sounds or notes when struck.

tempos
The rhythms and pace of music.

vaudeville
Live stage performances of singing, dancing, and a variety of other acts.

TO LEARN MORE

BOOKS

Fuhrer, Margaret. *American Dance: The Complete Illustrated History*. Minneapolis: Voyageur Press, 2014.

Tieck, Sarah. *Dancing*. Minneapolis: ABDO, 2013.

Van der Linde, Laurel. *So, You Want to Be a Dancer? The Ultimate Guide to Exploring the Dance Industry*. Hillsboro, OR: Beyond Words, 2015.

NOTE TO EDUCATORS

Visit **www.focusreaders.com** to find lesson plans, activities, links, and other resources related to this title.

INDEX

Answer Key: 1. Answers will vary; **2.** Answers will vary; **3.** C; **4.** B; **5.** B; **6.** A